I0659586

Copyright © 2025 Noelyn Whea
ISBN: 979-8-9990314-7-1

All rights reserved. No part of this publication may be reproduced, distributed, or transmitted in any form or by any means, including photocopying, recording, or other electronic or mechanical methods, without the prior written permission of the publisher, except in the case of brief quotations embodied in reviews and certain other non-commercial uses permitted by the copyright law.

Published in the United States, an imprint of Sweetbean books

The only source of knowledge is experience

-Albert Einstein

By Design

The system knows what it is doing and has

decided that knowing is not dangerous.

Chapter One

The meeting did not require preparation.

That was how it had been framed.

No materials were circulated in advance. No urgency flagged the invitation. Attendance was described as recommended, a word that carried just enough weight to ensure presence without implying consequence.

The room had been booked for ninety minutes.

It would not take that long.

They arrived separately.

Not by instruction—by habit.

Each entered with the same measured pace, coats removed before being asked, badges settling back into place with quiet familiarity. Their clothing fell within a narrow range of variation: structured jackets, soft collars, neutral fabrics designed to move without sound. Nothing stiff. Nothing expressive. Shoes that made no sharp report against the floor.

They took their seats without negotiation.

The table was already warm when they arrived.

Light filtered through a high pane of treated glass, diffused to soften edges and discourage shadow. The plants along the far wall were healthy in the way cultivated things often are trimmed, resilient, unlikely to surprise anyone. Their leaves caught the light without reflecting it.

Six people sat.

They knew one another by role more than name.

No one reached for a slate immediately. Hands rested on the table or folded loosely in laps. Posture was attentive without tension, bodies angled slightly inward, as if the room itself expected agreement.

This was not a meeting where documentation would be generated.

That work had already been done elsewhere.

The coordinator began without ceremony.

They did not stand. "Thank you for coming," they said. "I'll keep this brief." Their voice was even, practiced, carrying just far enough to fill the room without echo. When they gestured, it was with one hand only, palm down, as if smoothing a surface. A series of metrics appeared on the shared display. Trend lines. Stabilization curves. Resolution times. All of them improving. No one leaned forward. "We're seeing sustained alignment across sectors," the coordinator continued. "Disruption incidents are down. Completion rates are holding. Feedback remains within expected variance." No one objected. These numbers were familiar. They had been moving this way for some time.

An administrator leaned back slightly, hands folded.

The movement was subtle but visible, the signal of confidence rather than retreat.

"That tracks," she said. "Repositioning protocols have reduced strain on the outer tiers. We're hearing fewer escalation requests."

She spoke without emphasis, eyes remaining on the display.

A policymaker nodded once, slowly. "Risk exposure is down as well. Early interventions are preventing secondary effects."

A technocrat adjusted the display, enlarging a subsection with two fingers. His sleeve pulled back just enough to reveal a plain wristband, no markings, no time displayed.

"Efficiency gains remain consistent," he said.

"Where friction appears, it's localized. Manageable."

The word settled comfortably.

There was a pause.

Not uncertainty.

Consideration.

Several people shifted their weight at once, chairs responding with a soft, unified sound. The coordinator glanced around the table, then spoke again.

"There has been some discourse," they said, "regarding intentionality."

No one reacted.

The term was not new. It surfaced periodically, usually when internal language drifted too close to description.

"In what sense?" the administrator asked, neutrally.

The coordinator chose their phrasing with care. "There's an emerging perception," they said, "that current outcomes are being framed as incidental. Emergent. Unplanned."

The policymaker frowned slightly, not in concern, but in calculation. "They're not wrong."

"Not entirely," the coordinator agreed. "But the distinction matters."

The technocrat folded his hands on the table.

The gesture brought his fingers together precisely, knuckles aligned.

"We should be clear internally," he said. "These outcomes are not incidental."

The room absorbed the sentence without disturbance.

No one reached to soften it.

No one challenged it.

"Design doesn't imply malice," the administrator said after a moment. "It implies responsibility."

She shifted forward again, returning to the table.

"And foresight," the policymaker added. "Which we had."

"Still have," the coordinator said.

They returned their attention to the display.

A new set of metrics appeared. Predictive models. Load distribution forecasts.

Threshold tolerances.

"What matters," the coordinator said, "is that the system remains functional. That outcomes remain stable. The question of intent doesn't alter performance."

"It may alter perception," the administrator said.

"Yes," the coordinator replied. "Which is why this conversation stays here."

No one disagreed.

There was no sense of secrecy in the room. Only scope.

The distinction between internal clarity and external narrative had long been understood.

The policymaker glanced at the time.

"If the outcomes are acceptable," he said, "then the distinction is academic."

The coordinator nodded. "That's our position."

They stood.

Chairs slid back in near unison. Jackets were lifted, smoothed, put on. No one rushed. No one lingered. The meeting concluded as it had begun, quietly, efficiently, without leaving a trace that would require explanation later.

As they filed out, the display dimmed automatically, returning the room to its neutral state.

The plants continued to grow.

The system, having acknowledged itself, returned to maintenance.

Outside the room, the day proceeded as designed.

Chapter Two

The notice arrived while the kettle was still heating. It appeared on Rai's wall display as a courtesy band, thin, pale, easy to miss if you were already moving. She wiped her hands on a towel and stood there long enough for the text to finish resolving.

Routing Update Implemented.

Below it, smaller:

No action required.

Rai poured the water anyway. The kettle clicked off with a familiar finality. Steam lifted and vanished against the vent.

She read the notice again.

Routing updates happened often enough that she had learned not to read into them. The system adjusted. People adapted. That was the rhythm. The display dimmed slightly, interpreting her stillness as acknowledgement.

Outside, the morning had the flat clarity of managed weather.

Light arrived evenly. The street was already awake but not crowded, movement flowing along predictable lines.

Rai joined it.

She noticed the change at the third intersection.

The crossing signal lagged longer than usual, holding her with a small group she didn't recognize. When it finally changed, the pedestrian flow bent left instead of forward, guided by temporary barriers that looked permanent enough to trust.

No one complained.

The detour added two minutes.

At the transit hub, the platform assignment had shifted.

Rai scanned the board, recalculating out of habit. The new route would get her there. Later. She stepped onto the marked path, shoes striking the floor in time with the people around her.

The system was good at this.

It made changes feel like preferences.

At work, the day unfolded without interruption.

Her tasks arrived pre-sorted, priority flags already resolved. She completed them efficiently, pausing only once when a summary felt oddly smooth, its edges too clean.

She dismissed the thought.

The system did not reward overattention.

Midday brought a second notice.

This one arrived on her slate, tucked beneath a reminder about hydration.

Community Flow Optimization Complete.

Rai frowned, just briefly.

Community updates were usually posted publicly.

This one had been addressed to her directly.

She checked the details.

There were none.

On her way home, she tried to take her usual route.

The request did not deny her.

It paused.

A prompt appeared:

Please select an alternate path to support balanced circulation.

Rai hesitated.

The pause stretched just long enough to feel like a choice.

She selected the suggested route.

The alternate street was quieter, its storefronts dimmer, foot traffic thinner. She passed a familiar café and realized she had not been there in weeks.

The realization arrived without urgency.

She had not been prevented from going.

She had simply stopped being routed past it.

At home, the wall display glowed softly.

Another notice waited.

Thank you for your flexibility.

Rai laughed once, surprised by the sound.

Flexibility had always been one of her strengths.

She set her bag down and sat at the small table by the window. Outside, the street moved steadily, people arriving where they were meant to be.

The kettle was still warm.

She poured herself another cup.

The day had gone well.

Nothing had gone wrong.

Later, when she tried to recall how she had spent her time, the hours felt evenly distributed, difficult to distinguish.

She did not think about the meeting she would never know had happened.

She slept.

The system logged a successful adjustment.

Chapter Three

The change did not arrive as a notice.

It arrived as ease.

Rai woke before her alarm and did not mind. The light at the window had already adjusted to the hour, pale and even, promising a day without interruption. Her wall display offered the morning summary, weather steady, transit optimal, no advisories requiring attention.

She stood and dressed without deliberation.

Her clothes were clean, neutral, suited to movement. Nothing tugged or pinched. The fabric made no sound when she crossed the room.

At work, her slate opened to a simplified queue.

Fewer items. Longer windows. The kind of schedule that implied trust.

A banner appeared briefly at the top of the screen:

Assignment Alignment Confirmed.

It vanished before she could tap it.

The first case required only verification.

The second, a summary check.

The third arrived already resolved, her role reduced to acknowledgment. She hesitated with her finger hovering above the finalize field, the old habit tugging at her—read once more, feel for weight, locate the edge.

The prompt pulsed softly.

She finalized.

By midmorning, a colleague stopped at her desk.

Not to ask a question.

To thank her.

"Things have been smoother lately," they said. "Your adjustments really helped."

Rai nodded, unsure what adjustments they meant.

The gratitude lingered anyway.

At lunch, she noticed the table assignments had shifted.

She was seated near the window now, with people who spoke easily about light things, weekend plans, preferred routes, a new place that had opened along a corridor she no longer took.

She listened.

She laughed at the right moments.

Across the room, she saw someone she used to sit with, their table angled just far enough away to make interruption awkward.

She did not move.

In the afternoon, a message arrived marked **Optional**.

Professional Development Opportunity

It outlined a short program focused on *process continuity* and *stakeholder reassurance*.

Participation would reduce cognitive load and improve long-term placement stability.

Rai scrolled to the end.

The confirmation button waited, already highlighted.

She closed the message.

It reopened later.

When she left work, the exit corridor guided her toward the quieter street. The one with fewer storefronts. The one that led home without temptation.

The café she used to pass sat dark at this hour, its windows reflecting the street back at itself.

She paused.

The pause registered.

Nothing followed.

At home, the wall display greeted her with a soft tone.

Housing Optimization Notice

She read more carefully this time.

Due to improved alignment and to support balanced circulation, her residence would be reassigned within the week. The new location offered enhanced quiet, increased efficiency, and reduced transit variance.

No action was required.

Rai sat on the edge of the bed.

The room felt unchanged. Her belongings were where she had left them. The air moved steadily through the vent.

She imagined the new place.

Quieter.

Farther.

A message chimed on her slate.

From a name she had not seen in some time.

It did not open automatically.

Rai stared at the notification until the screen dimmed, interpreting her stillness as fatigue.

She did not tap it.

That night, she packed a box without meaning to.

Not everything.

Just the items closest to hand.

She labeled it **BOOKS**.

The word looked larger than it needed to be.

In bed, the quiet settled around her like a blanket.

Comfortable. Heavy.

She tried to recall the last time a day had asked

something of her.

The memory did not come.

In the morning summary, a new line appeared.

Relocation Prepared.

Below it:

Thank you for your flexibility.

Rai closed her eyes.

The system had not taken anything from her.

It had simply moved the rest of the world a little

farther away.

The adjustment logged as successful.

Interlude I

The system did not announce itself as control.

It introduced itself as assistance.

Most people encountered it first as convenience.

Information arrived without being requested.

Adjustments occurred before inconvenience could

register. The environment learned preferences

quickly enough that preference felt unnecessary.

Light shifted with the hour.

Transit aligned with movement.

Weather advisories appeared only when deviation

was statistically relevant.

Silence was preserved whenever possible.

No single interface governed these functions.

They were embedded.

In walls that updated when no one was looking. In

floors that guided circulation through subtle

resistance. In panels that dimmed once

acknowledgment was inferred.

The system did not require attention.

It interpreted it.

Users were not asked to confirm accuracy.

Feedback was inferred through compliance

metrics: pauses accepted, routes followed,

prompts dismissed or engaged.

Stillness was logged as satisfaction.

Deviation, when it occurred, was framed as fatigue.

Design standards emphasized non-intrusion.

Notifications avoided urgency unless delay posed

measurable risk. Visual language favored neutral

contrast. Audio cues were softened to prevent

stress accumulation.

The system learned quickly which individuals

responded best to reassurance.

It adjusted accordingly.

Control was never described as such.

The language favored balance, flow, optimization.

A successful day was defined as one that required no correction.

A successful citizen was one who did not need to ask where they were being guided.

Oversight occurred through aggregation.

No single actor monitored outcomes in full. Each domain evaluated performance within scope and reported stability upward. When indicators aligned, no further review was required.

This was considered ethical.

The system did not conceal its presence.

It simply made itself unremarkable.

And when people stopped noticing how much of their day arrived pre-arranged,

that was logged as trust.

The system continued to update.

It always did.

(End.)

Chapter Four

The new apartment was quieter.

That was the first thing Rai noticed.

Not the size. Not the layout. The quiet.

The building sat farther from the transit line, its entrance angled away from the main street. The lobby smelled faintly of cleaning solution and something mineral, like stone after rain. No music played. No announcements surfaced.

The wall panel by the door acknowledged her presence with a soft illumination, then dimmed.

Welcome.

No name followed.

Rai moved through the space slowly.

The furniture had been arranged according to efficiency guidelines, clear pathways, optimal light exposure, surfaces at rest height. Her belongings arrived already placed, the box labeled BOOKS stacked neatly beside the shelf it would occupy.

She touched the box but did not open it.

From the window, she could see a portion of the city she did not recognize.

The buildings were similar enough to feel familiar, but the angles were wrong. Streets curved where she expected them to meet. Foot traffic moved steadily but without overlap, people passing one another without interruption.

No one lingered.

Her slate chimed.

Relocation Complete.

Below it:

We hope you find the quite supportive.

Rai closed the slate.

That evening, she went for a walk.

The route suggested itself before she reached the door. She followed it out of habit, then realized she could not recall choosing it.

Halfway down the block, she slowed.

The itch returned.

Not sharp. Not urgent.

Persistent.

She tried to change direction. The street allowed it. But the lighting shifted ahead, softening the alternate path, drawing her back toward the recommended curve. The resistance was subtle enough to feel like preference. Rai stopped. The pause registered. Nothing followed.

She stood there longer than necessary, letting the moment stretch.

People passed her, unbothered. The system did not intervene. It did not need to.

The itch spread, settling beneath her skin like static.

She turned down the darker street.

The light behind her dimmed.

Ahead, the path narrowed, storefronts closing earlier here, windows reflecting her movement back at her in fragments.

Her heart rate ticked upward.

Not fear.

Effort.

At the end of the block, the street opened into a small square. Unoptimized. The ground was uneven. A bench sat crooked beneath a tree that had grown without guidance.

Two people argued quietly near a closed kiosk, their voices overlapping, unsmoothed.

Rai breathed out.

The itch eased.

She sat on the bench.

The surface was cold. The noise was inconsistent. A child laughed somewhere nearby, the sound sharp and unfiltered.

Rai felt something settle into place.

Not relief.

Recognition.

Her slate vibrated.

Route deviation detected.

Below it:

Are you safe?

Rai did not answer.

She remained seated until the light changed naturally, without instruction.

When she finally stood, the square looked the same.

Nothing had corrected itself.

Back in the apartment, the quiet pressed in again.

Supportive. Efficient.

Rai opened the box of books.

The smell of paper rose up, uneven and real. She pulled one free and sat on the floor with her back against the wall.

The wall panel dimmed, interpreting her stillness as rest.

She read until her eyes ached.

Later, as she lay in bed, the itch returned, not unbearable, but present.

This time, she did not try to smooth it away.

She let it stay.

Somewhere in the system, a deviation remained unclosed.

Interlude II

Deviations were not defined as errors.

They were defined as delays in alignment.

A deviation occurred when an individual's movement, attention, or response pattern diverged from projected flow beyond acceptable tolerance.

Most deviations resolved themselves.

People corrected course without instruction.

When they did not, the system intervened gently.

Deviations were categorized by type:

- **Navigational** (route variation, pause extension, unanticipated linger)
- **Cognitive** (incomplete confirmation, delayed response, unresolved focus)
- **Environmental** (preference for unoptimized space, noise tolerance variance)

Each category carried a recommended response.

Low-impact deviations required no action.

They were logged and monitored for recurrence.

A single deviation indicated curiosity.

Multiple deviations indicated fatigue.

Neither required correction.

Sustained deviations prompted outreach. Not enforcement. Support. Language templates emphasized reassurance: *Are you comfortable? Have your needs changed?* We noticed a pause and wanted to ensure continuity. The word pause tested well. Closure was achieved when:

- the individual resumed recommended
- patterns deviation frequency dropped
- below threshold stillness was re-established

Closure did not require explanation.

It required compliance.

In rare cases, deviations persisted.

These were flagged as **Unresolved**.

Unresolved deviations were not failures.

They were risks.

Risk was mitigated through proximity adjustment,

schedule smoothing, or role realignment.

If necessary, environmental quiet was increased.

Isolation was not indicated.

Distance was preferred.

The system did not punish deviation.

It absorbed it.

And when absorption proved insufficient,

it narrowed the conditions under which deviation

could occur.

An unresolved deviation remained open until

resolved.

Open deviations were reviewed periodically.

No timeline was assigned.

Stability was the priority.

(End.)

Chapter Five

The outreach arrived midmorning.

Not as an alert.

As a check-in.

Rai noticed it because it did not insist.

A small icon rested at the edge of her slate, neither urgent nor dismissible, the color tuned to recede if ignored. She finished reading the page in front of her before acknowledging it.

The icon brightened, just enough.

Support Contact Available

Below it:

We noticed a pause.

No timestamp.

No location.

No accusation.

Rai tapped once.

A window opened, not full-screen, not private. The background of her workspace remained visible, steadying. The voice that followed was warm without familiarity.

"Hello, Rai," it said. "Thank you for making time."

It did not ask how she was.

"I'm fine," Rai said anyway.

The voice accepted this.

"We believed you might be," it replied. "This isn't about concern. It's about continuity."

The word settled between them.

The voice explained the purpose of the contact carefully.

It had observed a deviation.

Not a problem.

A variation.

"These things happen," the voice said. "Especially during periods of transition. Relocation, schedule smoothing, reduced noise exposure." Rai listened. The list described her life accurately.

"We wanted to ensure the adjustments are still serving you," the voice continued. "Sometimes what begins as supportive can become misaligned. We correct early to prevent fatigue."

"Correct?" Rai asked.

The voice smiled audibly.

"Recalibrate," it said. "If necessary."

A pause followed.

Rai felt it register.

She said nothing.

"Can you tell me," The voice asked gently, "what drew you to that space?"

It did not name the square.

41

It did not name the street.

It did not need to.

Rai searched for an answer that would not sound unreasonable.

"I was walking," she said.

"Yes," the voice agreed. "And then?"

"I kept walking."

Another pause.

Longer this time.

"We want to support your autonomy," the voice said. "Within conditions that keep you well."

Rai recognized the phrasing.

Autonomy had always come with a modifier.

"Did I do something wrong?" she asked.

"No," the voice said immediately. "Nothing wrong occurred."

The certainty was reassuring.

"And nothing needs to be addressed?" Rai asked.

"Not if this was an isolated experience," the voice replied. "Many people seek novelty briefly after relocation. It resolves on its own."

A small panel appeared at the bottom of the window.

Optional Supportive Measures

Quiet enhancements. Route reinforcement.

Schedule refinement.

Each option carried a brief description.

Each promised ease.

Rai did not select anything.

The panel waited.

"We don't require a decision now," the voice said.

"This is simply an invitation. Our goal is to keep things from becoming difficult."

Difficult.

The word landed where the itch had been.

"I like the quiet," Rai said.

"We know," the voice replied. "Your metrics indicate improved rest."

Rai closed her eyes.

"Is there a problem with wanting more?" she asked.

The voice did not answer immediately.

When it did, it spoke carefully.

"Wanting is not a problem," it said. "Unresolved wanting can be."

Another pause.

Rai felt the space around it narrow.

"We'll leave the options available," the voice said.

"You can engage them at any time. Or not at all. Either way, we're here."

The window dimmed slightly, signaling closure without ending the connection.

"Thank you for your openness," the voice added.

The interface returned to Rai's work.

The icon disappeared.

Nothing had been decided.

Later, as she walked home along the recommended route, Rai felt the itch again.

It did not demand action.

It asked a question.

Not *what do you want?*

But *how much difficulty are you willing to carry?*

Somewhere in the system, the deviation remained open.

Interlude III

Artifact Review:

Closed Item

The file surfaced during routine reconciliation.

Not flagged.

Not urgent.

It appeared because the system was clearing redundancies.

Name: NAVI

Role: Peripheral Review (Former)

Status: Reassigned

No date accompanied the reassignment.

Dates were unnecessary once outcomes stabilized.

The artifact consisted of fragments.

Not records.

Annotations. Marginal notes. Partial transcripts that had never been finalized.

Material unsuitable for aggregation.

The system had retained them by default.

A reviewer paused.

This was not required.

The pause registered as negligible.

The annotations referenced weight.

Not metaphorical.

Operational.

Mentions of delay framed as *completion sensitivity*.

Notes on cases closed *before settlement*. A

recurring phrase appeared across unrelated

entries:

Allow time for the body.

The phrase did not correspond to any active

framework.

A cross-reference populated automatically.

Related Impact: Low

Transmission: Contained

Residual Influence: Minimal

The system recommended closure.

The reviewer scanned the final entry.

A mentorship log.

Language divergence noted.

No corrective action recorded.

Outcome: Integration successful.

The artifact should have been archived.

Instead, it lingered.

The reviewer felt a faint irritation, difficult to place.

Not concern.

Misalignment.

They hovered over the finalize field.

The cursor waited.

Another panel opened, unprompted.

Deviation Status: Open

No subject attached.

The reviewer closed the file.

Not finalized. Not archived.

Just closed.

The system logged the action as neutral.

A closed item reopened later required no

justification.

Elsewhere, a deviation remained unresolved.

The system adjusted around it.

It always did.

(End.)

Chapter Six

The difficulty did not arrive as resistance.

It arrived as residue.

Rai noticed it first in her work.

Cases that should have resolved cleanly began to leave behind a sensation she could not name. Not doubt. Not concern. A faint afterpressure, as if something had been closed too early and was still pressing from the other side.

She reread summaries she had already finalized.

Nothing was wrong.

One file caught slightly on opening.

The delay was less than a second.

Enough to register.

The header populated without metadata.

No name.

No date.

Just a classification marker she had not seen in active use.

Peripheral Residual

Rai frowned.

The category was deprecated.

She scrolled.

The contents were fragmentary. Marginal notes embedded between standard fields. Phrases without resolution. Language that had not been normalized.

She felt the itch surface immediately.

One line repeated across unrelated sections:

Allow time for the body.

Rai's breath caught.

The phrase was not indexed.

It should not have been there.

She searched the internal glossary.

No match.

She searched policy archives.

Before bed, Jonah set his alarm.

The panel suggested a slightly later wake time to support rest continuity.

He accepted.

Somewhere nearby, a variable held.

It did not resolve.

It absorbed pressure without converting it into data.

The system adjusted around it.

As designed.

(End.)

Rai felt a memory stir without image.

A voice, once.

Not instruction.

Orientation.

The sense that weight was something you stayed with, not something you moved past.

Her chest tightened.

She closed the file.

Not   finalized.   Not

archived.   Just

closed.

The system logged the action as neutral.

No follow-up occurred.

That evening, walking home, the itch followed her more insistently.

She deviated from the recommended route without noticing the decision.

The street did not correct her.

She passed the unoptimized square again.

The bench sat where it had before.

The tree dropped a leaf at her feet, uncounted.

Rai stood there, the phrase echoing in her mind.

Allow time for the body.

She understood something then.

The system was not incomplete.

It was impatient.

At home, the wall display brightened.

We noticed a recurrence.

Below it:

Would you like support?

Rai did not answer.

Later, as she lay in bed, the residue settled.

Not uncomfortable.

Present.

She did not try to resolve it.

She let it remain.

Somewhere in the system, an artifact had found a place to rest.

And somewhere else, a deviation learned how to wait.

Chapter Seven

The opportunity arrived with congratulations.

Rai received the message just after midday, when her queue was light and the building had settled into its quiet rhythm. The slate chimed once pleasant, unobtrusive and displayed a banner edged in a color reserved for advancement.

Placement Expansion Available

Below it:

You have been identified for increased scope.

She read the message twice.

The language was careful. Commendatory without excess. It praised consistency, adaptability, and her demonstrated capacity to maintain continuity during periods of transition.

There was no mention of deviation.

The opportunity outlined new access.

A broader review range. Increased discretion. Fewer checkpoints. The ability to move between classifications without triggering secondary oversight.

Freedom, reframed as trust.

Rai felt the itch tighten.

Not flare.

Condense.

She accepted the briefing.

A window opened, brighter than her usual interface but not intrusive. The voice returned, not the same one as before, but similar enough to feel intentional.

"We want to recognize your stability," it said. "Not everyone adjusts as well as you have."

Rai said nothing.

"With expanded placement," the voice continued, "you'll encounter material that hasn't been fully harmonized. Transitional content. Legacy language. Residuals."

The word lingered.

"You'll be asked to exercise judgment," the voice said. "To resolve what no longer aligns."

Resolve.

Rai's fingers curled against the edge of the desk.

"Support will remain available," the voice added.

"But we trust you to know when intervention is

unnecessary."

The implication settled quietly.

A panel appeared.

Access Acknowledgment Required

Below it, a single line:

Expanded scope may increase exposure to

unresolved material.

No risks were listed.

No consequences named.

Rai closed the window.

She stood and walked to the edge of the floor,

where the glass overlooked the lower levels of the

city. From here, movement looked smooth.

Predictable. Beautiful in its efficiency.

She imagined herself inside those flows,
redirected, protected.
She imagined stepping between them.
Her slate pulsed softly.
Waiting.

She thought of the phrase.
Allow time for the body.
It did not fit anywhere in the briefing.
That, she realized, was the point.

Rai returned to her desk.
She reopened the acknowledgment panel.
The system had framed this as opportunity.
It was also a test.

If she accepted, she would gain access and inherit
responsibility for closing what lingered.
If she declined, the deviation would remain open.
Visible.

Her finger hovered.

The system waited.

Outside, a cloud passed briefly across the sun,

shifting the light in the room without instruction.

Rai noticed.

She did not accept.

She did not decline.

She let the panel remain.

Open.

Somewhere, a metric stalled.

Somewhere else, a pathway remained unfinalized.

The opportunity did not expire.

It adjusted.

And the system learned that Rai could hold weight

without resolving it.

That, too, was logged.

Chapter Eight

The meeting was framed as optional.

Rai knew better.

The invitation arrived without urgency, embedded between routine notices, its language carefully neutral.

Alignment Conversation Available

Below it:

Your perspective would be valuable.

No deadline.

No consequence listed.

Rai accepted.

The confirmation felt immediate, as though the system had been waiting.

The room was not the one from the briefings. It was smaller. Lower. Designed for proximity rather than overview. The chairs were arranged at equal distance from the table, which held nothing at its center. The light was warmer here, the air marginally heavier.

Someone had decided this mattered. The facilitator arrived already seated. They stood when Rai entered, smiled, gestured toward the chair opposite. "Thank you for coming," they said. "We appreciate your willingness to engage." Engage.

"This isn't a review," the facilitator continued. "It's a conversation. We're interested in how things are landing." Landing. Rai sat.

The facilitator's clothing matched the room, soft lines, neutral color, nothing that would interrupt attention. Their hands rested openly on the table. "You've been identified as someone with a high tolerance for complexity," they said. "That's a strength."
Rai felt the weight of the sentence settle.

"Complexity can be costly," the facilitator added gently. "Not just for systems. For people."

Rai waited.

"We want to make sure you're not carrying more than you need to," they said. "Sometimes our definitions lag behind lived experience. When that happens, we adjust."

Adjust.

Rai looked at the table.

"There are things that don't fit," she said.

The facilitator nodded. "There always are."

"But they're treated like errors," Rai said. "Or fatigue."

"Because they often are," the facilitator replied. "From our perspective."

A pause.

The facilitator did not fill it.

They were listening.

"I don't think the system is wrong," Rai said slowly. "I think it's unfinished."

The word hung between them.

Unfinished.

The facilitator's smile did not falter.

"Completion is a process," they said. "We don't aim for finality. We aim for stability."

Rai felt the itch rise.

She did not smooth it.

"There are parts of people you can't optimize away," she said. "They come back. As pressure."

The facilitator folded their hands.

"We're aware," they said. "Which is why we offer options."

A panel on the table illuminated.

Not a screen.

A surface.

Consent Framework – Individual Pathway

"This is not a demand," the facilitator said. "It's an opportunity. To align your experience with our capacities."

Rai read.

The language was careful. Generous. It acknowledged complexity. It promised agency.

It also asked for agreement.

"If you consent," the facilitator continued, "we can expand support. Refine definitions. Integrate your perspective more fully." "And if I don't?" Rai asked.

The facilitator did not answer immediately.

When they did, their voice remained warm.

"Then we continue as we are," they said. "With appropriate boundaries."

Boundaries.
Rai understood what that meant.

She looked up.
"Who decides when it's finished?" she asked.
The facilitator met her gaze.
"We do," they said. "Together."

Rai sat back.
She thought of the square. The bench. The phrase that had no category.
Allow time for the body.

"I'm not ready," she said.
The facilitator nodded.
"Read it," they said. "Sit with it. There's no rush."

The panel dimmed.

The meeting concluded without resolution.

As Rai left the room, the system updated several models.

Not alarms.

Assumptions.

The deviation remained open.

But now it had a shape.

And the system, for the first time, had been forced to meet it.

(End.)

Final Interlude

The route opened earlier than expected.

Jonah noticed it on his way home.

The evening corridor usually dense at this hour, had thinned. Signals favored his pace. The crossing cleared before he reached it. The train arrived without delay, doors opening almost as soon as he stepped onto the platform.

He felt a small, unearned relief.

He hadn't changed anything.

He still left work at the same time. Still took the same path. Still kept his head down, grateful when days asked little of him.

But lately, the city seemed to meet him halfway.

At home, his wall panel updated quietly.

Flow Adjustment Successful.

Below it:

Thank you for your flexibility.

Jonah smiled, just slightly. It was good to be noticed.

Elsewhere, the system logged a redistribution.

Not an escalation.

A refinement.

Pressure had accumulated in one area beyond optimal tolerance. Rather than resolve it directly, the system adjusted surrounding variables.

Load shifted.

Transit eased.

Latency reduced across adjacent paths.

Jonah cooked dinner without interruption.

The kitchen light softened as the sun set. Noise from the street remained low. He ate standing at the counter, then sat, feeling pleasantly tired in a way that suggested the day had been used well. He did not think about why it had felt easier.

The system did.

An unresolved deviation remained active.

Classification updated:

High-Impact Complexity

Containment Strategy: Deferred

Stability Outcome: Positive (Distributed)

No subject name attached.

Names were unnecessary at this stage.

Jonah opened a book he had been meaning to finish.

The words came easily tonight. His attention did not drift. When he paused, it felt natural, chosen.

He thought, briefly, that things were improving.

The system confirmed this assessment.

Aggregate satisfaction indicators rose marginally.

Noise complaints declined. Route congestion eased in three neighboring sectors.

The deviation remained open.

It no longer needed to be addressed.

It was doing work.

Before bed, Jonah set his alarm.

The panel suggested a slightly later wake time to support rest continuity.

He accepted.

Somewhere nearby, a variable held.

It did not resolve.

It absorbed pressure without converting it into data.

The system adjusted around it.

As designed.

(End.)

Epilogue

The message arrived without urgency.

No alert tone. No priority flag. It appeared in the queue the way weather does—already there by the time it was noticed.

Review Available.

Rai did not open it at first.

She had learned, by then, that immediacy was a form of instruction.

Outside, the city continued to function. Routes adjusted. Loads redistributed. Satisfaction indicators held steady. The deviation she represented no longer registered as friction. It had been incorporated into surrounding patterns, its presence accounted for without being resolved. Stability metrics improved.

When Rai finally accessed the review, the language was careful.

It acknowledged complexity.

It thanked her for continued engagement.

It noted that certain processes had been refined as a result of her persistence.

No apology was offered. None was required.

At the bottom of the document was a section she had not seen before.

Not a warning.

Not a directive.

A proposal.

The terms were reasonable. That was the unsettling part.

They accounted for her concerns. They recognized the limits she had exposed. They even named uncertainty as a shared condition.

Participation was optional.

Support would continue regardless.

Nothing would be taken away.

Rai read the terms twice.

Then a third time.

She noticed what was not specified.

The duration.

The scope.

The cost.

Outside her window, the lights adjusted as evening settled in. Somewhere, a route eased. Somewhere else, a delay lengthened. The system moved around its variables with practiced grace.

It had learned how to live with her.

Now it was asking something different.

At the end of the proposal, a single line waited.

Do you agree to proceed?

No countdown followed.

No consequence was named.

The question did not hurry her.

It did not need to.

Rai closed the document.

She did not decline.

She did not accept.

For now, she let the question remain.

Somewhere in the system, a new status registered.

Pending Consent.

www.ingramcontent.com/pod-product-compliance
Lightning Source LLC
Chambersburg PA
CBHW060443260626
47161CB00005B/2052